Return To 'Ouja: After the Deluge

A Wise Report To A Wise Minister By A Wise Citizen

Hichem Karoui

Global East-West (London)

Contents

Part Two:
Glorious Days in the Golden Age

Book (8)

The Morning of the Mogul
A wise report to a wise minister by a
wise citizen
(A serialised novel)

Return To 'Ouja

After the Deluge

Volumes in this series published by Global East-West (London)

Dedication

To the memory of Nana ...
Beloved mother...
You are always in my heart.
May you rest in eternal peace.

Notes

Note of the Publisher

This is Mister Bassam Bourasin's admitted report as a citizen of His republic. He didn't give it a name. He initially addressed it to the Interior Ministry. Instead, it landed on my desk. I publish it as is, with no major changes to its form or content. However, because the report is around 800 pages long, it will be serialised. Here is book Eight: Return to 'Ouja.

Other volumes will soon follow in Part Three of the series.

I also have to notice that this is a translation. The first draft was written in Arabic. The author had no intention of publishing it. In any case, it is understandably unpublishable in the country... for the same reasons that silence any samizdat.

Hichem Karoui

Note of the Author

All of the individuals in my story, as well as the country, are not made up. However, even if some characters claim to be more fictive or strange, crazier or more foolish than others, they are not required to justify their location. My country can be found

throughout the Arab world. Whatever name people give it, you won't notice a difference if you pay attention.
Bassam Bourasin

"Nobody   did
a   secret
deal

Nobody   was
for sale

Nobody bent
the rules at all

And   nobody

went to jail

And all of
them were
honest men

As white as
driven snow

And lived on a
higher plane

And shat on
those below..."

Roger Woddis: All Clear

"And so, what could my sterile and uncouth genius beget but the tale of a dry, shrivelled, whimsical offspring, full of old fancies such as never entered another's brain — just what might be begotten in prison, where every discomfort is lodged and every dismal noise has its dwelling?"

Cervantes: Don Quixote (Prologue)

Chapter One

RETURN OF THE PRODIGAL SON

I painstakingly calculated the situation. I would have spent precisely five months, three days, seven hours, fifteen minutes, and thirty-three seconds in the vivarium dubbed - quite meaninglessly, in my opinion - jail. Indeed, it is hardly the most panegyrised location to visit and, once there, to remain in. So far from it, if it were indeed a State-owned hotel

- and neither Hassan nor I doubted it - it should grow more sociable for the gentlemen and less profligate for the beleaguered crooks and other scammers and psychopaths forced to cohabit under its ceilings. Otherwise, who would willingly forego the warmth of family life for a brief or a long stay out there? And if such an honourable institution were to be rejected by its prospective customers, it would be a major loss for the State and the future anti-state couvolutionists. The State would feel deprived of a good coercion and repression tool, and the anti-state militants of a Bastille for their dark conspiracies.

We must also know how to manage such a system because this is not just a place but a system.

• • • ● • ● • ● • ● • ● • ••

I am now a free man writing these words honestly from my house in 'Ouja, where I've been for three days mourning and, in my grief, enjoying an intimacy that I have almost forgotten while struggling with gloom, depression and shadows.

I did not come in the Director of Security's Mercedes but in a roaring Land Rover driven by a stylish chauffeur. As soon as we crossed the main and unique street of the hamlet, we were followed by hundreds of eyes. Well! 'Hundreds' is probably a euphemism in the present conditions. After the atrocious killing of so many residents, there aren't many people remaining to cheer on my achievement. The savage disaster has left lasting and horrible scars on the streets and the walls. The survivors are suffering indescribable trauma. A thick cloud of melancholy and sorrow has descended over the community. I'd never felt so out of place in my own house. Perhaps I am not an alien, but 'Ouja is getting curiously far from me. I barely recognised my home town. The metamorphosis is startling and terrible; the trauma has upset me since I arrived.

Nothing is more terrifying than the bizarre conclusion that you are not the person you have always believed you are or that the area where you have always lived seems not to be your hometown, as you thought! One thing is certain: either I'm not the real Bassam Bourasin, or 'Ouja isn't the real 'Ouja!

When the Land Rover approached

the main street, I spotted regular soldiers in raggy dirty uniforms and many small groups of armed militiamen striding on the sidewalks and parading around closed shops. They were much more similar to an army of invaders than to local citizens. There was a tank at the village's entrance, and I couldn't help but observe that the guys riding it weren't all clothed in military uniforms. Some of them were dressed in civilian clothing, like jellabas, dishdasha, and similar Arab robes, and I can't say they were spruce and clean. So far from it, they seemed uneven, with swarthy long-bearded cheeks, and looked like an army of half-starved shadows ready to attack you for no other reason than your face, which they did not like.

The driver glanced at me sidelong as I sat beside him, confused and stagnant.   "Those are our men," he said proudly. "The Revolutionary Militia. Look how happy they are. Authentic lions! They'd get the head of the Scoundrel, wouldn't they?"

I did not respond. I was grumpy not just because I was returning to the village to watch the effects of a boundless misfortune but also because I was morally and physically exhausted. In reality, the car did not come at seven o'clock to pick me up, as Hassan had promised, but the following morning. As a result, I had spent the night awake with anxiety swallowing me up, wondering whether anything had gone wrong. I had washed and shaved, changed my clothing, and waited in the cell for the driver. But nobody called me. It was the worst night I'd had since being locked up. Waves of despair rolled over the deserted cost of my soul. I couldn't even eat, and my grief became excruciating when, unexpectedly, the TV speaker declared that the members of the Scoundrel's army had committed a terrible atrocity in 'Ouja. All the inmates hurried to the TV set to watch the first pictures of the horrendous tragedy. I saw the depressing fate that doomed my community at once and couldn't see any further. So, disgusted and daunted, I averted my gaze from the screen. I didn't want to watch my mother and fiancée's bodies lancinated and ripped apart. I didn't have the energy to deal with it.

• • • • •• • ● • ● • ● • •

The news quickly spread across the cell. Dahdah finally approached me, sallow-faced and quivering with emotion. "My heartfelt condolences, brother. I just now learned of the tragedy that has befallen your family."

Suleiman Mughli came up and kissed me on the cheeks as well. Then he handed me a packet of his American smokes, which I declined, but he insisted: "You'll need it, man. You're going to see your hometown. It's a long trip."

So I grabbed the packet and started smoking idly. I've been smoking since that evening. It's like being contaminated with a virus — a sweet one that makes you think it is soothing. The Mughli would have given me more, but I flatly refused. The other inmates followed as soon as they heard the news, and when they finally returned to their usual routine, I was alone with Dahdah, who sat opposite me on the hard mattress at the bottom of the cell. "You know what they say around here," he said in my ear, approaching his chubby face.

I shook my head in denial.

– They say this is the filthy work of the Afghan and his cohort.

– What exactly do you mean? Who said that?

– Everybody. Did you miss the incredible coincidence? The day before the slaughter, the Afghan returned and negotiated the release of all his rabid dogs and recognised criminals imprisoned for life. They said they would be sent to another jail, although this was a lie. Those guys have absolutely nothing to lose, you understand? They most likely informed them, "We'll release you if you do whatever we tell you." Because they are inexcusable murderers serving life terms, it was an open door to freedom for them. They are perfectly capable of committing any genocide.

My thoughts were racing.

– Do you mean that the Afghan and those men are the true criminals that acted under the government's supervision? I said, shocked.

– Exactly, Dahdah said.

– I can't believe it. Why should they be so cruel to the people they pledged to protect?

– Who can tell? They may want to discourage the populace from supporting the ex-president by implying that he is only a chronic murderer who would not hesitate to provoke a genocide in his thirst for power.

It was a terrifying thought. Yet, there is no evidence to support it.

- These are rumours, I replied. The Afghan is not as free as you may think. The new administration would not let him go on a rampage at his leisure. What the heck? We're not in Afghanistan! I can tell you that the new administration is dead set on punishing the culprits, whomever they may be. I was chatting to the incoming Director of Security, one of us, this morning.

– Are you referring to Hassan? That guy was never one of my friends. A sycophant and opportunist who would sell even his mother for such a position! I used to read his crap at the time; it was insane! He had licked the boots of all the King's Ministers, and when they were knocked down, he didn't mind licking the shoes and bottoms of their successors. And he's surely putting his tongue deep into the depths of Islamist rulers right now. That guy got everyone. He was born to lick boots and butts!

– You are unfair, Dahdah. You

do not know the dude. He is a very capable politician, well-informed, and, most importantly, incredibly kind and humanist.

Dahdah grinned and mockingly replied:

– Kind and humanist like a snake, yeah! Then, with his hurdy-gurdy fiddling, he got you, my dear! You don't know those sharks as well as I do. Have you always lived happily in your village? The Capital is a whole other universe, brother. They are capable of anything, I can tell you.

– Dahdah, don't you act as if this blasted Capital was on another planet. I lived in a village, but I'm not a moron. I can still tell the difference between a good fellow and a scumbag. I'm not afraid to admit that I believe Hassan more than a rumour based on hearsay and assumptions. So I see no reason to suspect he's fooling me. He has no reason to do so.

– OK, trust him; but you should know he is a hypocrite. Hassan is no more an Islamist than Zorro or any of the scabrous little goons you see around here.

I'm not sure how Dahdah came to this conclusion, but he wasn't far off the mark. Nonetheless, I held to the assumption that President Abdelghaffar's soldiers had nothing to do with the savage massacre. If Hassan knew that his friends had killed my family, he would not even consider offering me the hand of his unique and cherished sister, let alone the promise of a medal. It makes no sense.

Frankenstein asked me in the shower room that afternoon, "I heard you're going to be released, is that true?"

– Who told you?

He laughed.

– There's nothing to hide here, lad. Is it a state secret?

– No, it isn't. Did you happen to see me with Hassan in the library?

– No, I didn't, but I was told you'd been babbling with that cop all morning. At the very least, he is not ungrateful since he does not forget his friends.

I remained mute, but he observed the fresh clothing I'd brought to the shower and added, "You're going back to your bank, it seems."

– I don't know just yet.

– Good luck! He exclaimed, then added, You won't forget your promise, will you?

– What? I said quickly and perhaps rashly. Are you kidding?

I pretended to object to the unthinkable thought of hiring a mobster at my bank. Despite my uneasy response, he went up and took me like a feather into his sturdy arms, exactly like the first day, but without the fury, and he cried airily, to the surprise of the inmates: "You chum, man of man!"

I couldn't say anything because I was taken aback, and I pushed him vainly as I glanced at his bald round head and frightful mask, sparkling in the faint light of the lamp that had been turned on although it was early afternoon. Then he took me to his chest and kissed my forehead, and I was overcome by his foul odour of tobacco and sweat, so I yelled out, "Put me on the floor, for God's sake!" "I suffer from vertigo."

But he held me over his head again and said, "That's a chum, man of man!"

And he kept me hovering about

the room like a small bird while the inmates cheered and applauded the 'chum, man of man' that I was. Then, finally, he relented and threw me on the ground. Thus, it was evident that he didn't aim to hurt me but rather to show his excitement, completely oblivious - the moron! - that I meant precisely the opposite of what he had just realised. But, knowing that despite his gorilla-like look, he is an expressive person, I did not dare to convey the actual meaning of my response and instead chose to let him celebrate his future 'career' at the bank rather than shatter his dream.

• • • • ● • ● ● • • •

Chapter Two

THOSE WHO DID NOT BOARD THE ARCH OF NOAH

AFTER FRANKENSTEIN, IT WAS the shrink's turn to take the stage. I was shaving in the courtyard when Mahmoud came in from the block, gently asking whether "Mister Bassam would have the obligation to accord five minutes of his time to Mr the social assistant."

– Yes, said I. I'll meet him as soon as I finish shaving.

Mahmoud left the courtyard

wearing the same sobbing bulldog expression he had in the library. Meanwhile, I noted that the barber was now using a VIP Fresh blade to shave me. Life is full of surprises! And he made sure I noticed it. To my stupefaction, he claimed that "shaving the scented beard of Mister Hassan's friend was not a great event that made his day."

I thanked him for the accolade, and he said, "It's an honour for me, Mr Bassam".

Now I have become Mr Bassam for Mahmoud and the barber. Both have been so rude to me. But life is in continual change as the power balance shifts from one side to another.

The barber lingered, then:

– May I ask you a small favour, sir?

I had anticipated it.

– I'm listening to you.

– I've been here for three years and three months. I've been condemned to four years in prison, and I'd be so grateful if you intervened to alleviate my suffering.

– Ah! I will talk to Hassan, but I can't guarantee anything.

He thanked me profusely. He took a small perfume flask from his pocket as he finished the job. He sprinkled its contents over my face, neck, and hair, gently rubbing them with his soaked palms, not forgetting to emphasise that 'the perfume was Parisian' and that the treatment was reserved exclusively for 'the most important personalities of the prison'.

• • • • •• • • • • •

When I entered the shrink's office,

spotless, tidy, and scented, I expected to see the same cold little guy, with the gruff voice and the silver-rimmed spectacles hanging over his nose, smoking cigarettes in a chain and admiring the small clouds of blue smoke he was producing. That was different from the guy I was looking at. Something had changed in him since our first interview. I was surprised that as soon as his orangutan secretary alerted him that I was in the anteroom, the shrink opened the gate and virtually pounced on me, all grin and honey, took my elbow gently, and ushered me into his office as if I were a longtime buddy or family member. Such a warm greeting from a guy I knew was highly persuaded of his superiority immediately stunned me. I observed that the framed poster of our former president decorating the wall had disappeared as he welcomed me to sit and instructed his orangutan to bring up two cups of tea. Instead, the poster was properly replaced by a larger photo of the new strong man: Abdelghani Abdelghaffar, who was not smiling, but just puzzling us with his enigmatic black glasses, which cleverly concealed the two small gems gazing freely behind them. Surprisingly, I'm just now getting used to our president's visage. I discovered that having a president with a double vision is rather empathetic, and it is likely good - for him as well as for us - to lead two nations instead of one, with two peoples, two armies, and a double of everything inside them, something like the arch of Noah.

Thus, the shrink was up to date and quite in line. He gave me a cigarette, which I accepted, lit it, and stated:

– How nice to see you again, Mr Bassam. How are things going for you?

I didn't answer. Didn't he know?

– You were happy with the work I assigned you. It was a courtesy I had never accorded a detainee since the first day. But I had a feeling you're different from the rest. Eh! I was correct.

– I appreciate it, sir.

– I always thought you were a good chap, and you proved it, right? I see you're thriving.

My fine suit had clearly pleased him since he had been looking at my clothing the whole time.

– I knew I was making a good investment when I offered you that job, Mr Bassam, he added before I responded. It was, indeed, an excellent investment...

He grinned as he rubbed his hands together. He was ecstatic.

– Excuse me, sir, but are you

talking about money? In fact, after working for about five months, I am still waiting to get my pay.

The shrink laughed as if I'd told him the most hilarious joke he'd ever heard. He laughed so heartfully that tears welled in his eyes, and he removed his spectacles to wipe them with a tissue. He chuckled even as the secretary returned, bearing the tray of tea, and stood up in the middle of the room, surprised and unsure of what to do next. Finally, he decided to place the tray on the desk, moved away, and, as if infected by his boss's unrestrained amusement, he burst out laughing and gripped his stomach with both hands. Then I couldn't hold back my laughter any longer, and while I didn't understand what had caused that sudden fury, I felt its idiotic thrill entering me wave after wave, and I broke out laughing, forgetting my grief. The situation's humour was immeasurably impulsive and enticing enough to keep me from questioning its logic. But, of course, it was nonsense since at least two of the three dudes in the room, including myself, had no idea why they were giggling. That lasted a considerable while, and when we eventually came to our senses, we looked at each other like three perfect fools, goggling and stupefied by our ridiculous performance. The first to stop laughing was the psy. He put on his spectacles and yelled at his assistant:

– What are you laughing at, double moron?

The secretary's chuckle immediately froze. Now he seemed paralysed, like an Iceman made up and left by the children.

– You brought the tea, didn't you?

The shrink continued. What are you waiting for now?

The poor secretary withdrew and locked the door without saying a word. Meanwhile, I had recomposed.

– I apologise to you, Mr Bassam, replied the shrink.

– Forget about it! I was also laughing.

– Yes, he mumbled. Mr Bassam, you strike me as a compassionate figure. I am delighted to have met you. I hope you remember us once you're outside.

He came to a halt. He hadn't summoned me only to spout this nonsense.

– I can't possibly forget you, sir. The days I spent in this establishment will not be forgotten quickly. But you didn't respond to my question, did you?

– Yes, you are correct. I would have gone on and on about the matter from the first day. I'm afraid there is no salary.

  – No pay?

  – In this place, none. The detainees' labour is benevolent. We don't reward them.

  That was the prison! Sur-exploiting all those people in diverse jobs while refusing to compensate them for their honest efforts! It was inequitable.

  – Then why did you summon me, sir?

  – I did not summon you, Mr Bassam. I just invited you for a cup of tea before you leave us.

  – Ah! It's so kind of you, sir.

  – Trust me, seeing a man I helped succeed gives me great pleasure. (pause) By the way, I'd like to ask you for a small favour.

  I was somewhat taken aback and inquired:

  – A favour from me, sir?

– Well... umm... Not from you, but from your friend, unless he is your relative.

I remembered the barber and almost inadvertently blurted:

– You too, sir?

Then, seeing his confusion and amazement at my response, I quickly added: - I'll do my best. I owe you that.

– Oh no, no, Mr Bassam. You don't owe me. I'm just counting on your kindness.

The hypocrite!

– In fact, it is not complicated, he went on. I've been assigned to this post for seventeen years. So you understand, It's grown so oppressively exhausting that I feel like any inmate here. I wish to be transferred to another department, and I'd like you to speak to the Chief of Security about my request.

Ah! Voila, voila! Now I see!

– Where do you wish to be transferred?

– Anywhere! But please, not to another prison. Various other departments in the Ministry may need experienced staff. Mr Bassam, I may be useful even at a bank.

– Really? And you want to be repositioned to a bank?

– Not necessarily a bank, but I would not turn it down. I don't know much about banking but I can work in the human resources service. Why not?

– Quite right. I completely get what you mean. I'll see what I can do.

The guy got overjoyed and spent at least five minutes thanking and rethanking me, even though I attempted to emphasise that I could not move him and that all I could do was talk it over with Hassan without guaranteeing anything. But he appeared to believe that I was capable of more than I dared to confess.

Finally, he recalled that my mother and fiancée had been slain in the terrible disaster of 'Ouja. He broke down in apologies and condolences and would mourn with me if I showed the least proclivity to shed hot tears for my dead. But I stayed silent.

I was perplexed when I left the shrink's office since he gave me much more authority than I had. He was not a very perceptive psychologist. He appeared to believe that I was Hassan's supervisor, even though I had no power over the Director of Security. How could I have? I'm at his mercy, not the other way around.

• • • • •• • • • • ••

Anyway, I'm back in 'Ouja, my beloved hamlet that the Barbarians had half-destroyed and ravaged; and I'm writing these words by candlelight since they hadn't yet restored the ruined electric and telephone lines.

My first day was agonising. The sun was scorching the countryside on this sweltering day. The chauffeur, a middle-aged guy with dark flashing eyes and a hooky nose, never stopped chatting in the vehicle. While my eyes searched the dismal panorama, with its gaping hillocks, scattered weeds, and musty stones, I listened to him barking listlessly. It's a desolate area of rough magnificent cliffs and harsh tawny flora, scorched by the sour acid sun's smouldering beams. It is a place that is so similar to its people that it is unnecessary to speculate on why such atrocities occur. We are as callous and ruthless as the land of our country.

Some of us are undoubtedly formed of its rocks and stones; they are tremendously insensitive and totally wry, if not depraved, in their love of blood and devastation. My own town has the odd name of 'Ouja! Why 'Ouja? Everyone understands the word's meaning: wry, not right, not straight! But not just one community that's off; it's the whole damned nation. At least, this is how any rational human being would see it. The country has gone insane with a cataleptic hunger for riches, power, and blood, as if this unholy trio is the dreadful destiny everyone will suffer now. Are we doomed forever? The discovery of oil and natural gas in our soil did not improve us; it made us greedy, mischievous, lecherous, materialistic, utterly selfish and evil. I missed the days when life in our nation was simple and quiet, as I was told.

Life lacked modern amenities, but at least people were still human, hospitable and generous. They didn't murder each other for no reason. This is a dreadful flaw, a modern-day tragedy.

I went to the cemetery with Mr Houssine, my ex-father-in-law. I directed the driver to Dalila's residence, a little bungalow on the outskirts of the community. We parked the Land Rover and started walking. I knocked on the door and waited, my pulse pounding and unsure what to say in such a difficult situation. The driver was hesitant to attend, but I assured him it was just like my house and that he was welcome. As a result, he accompanied me and stood by my side.

I knocked again, loudly, since I knew they wouldn't hear me if they were listening to the radio or the TV. Finally, after a time, the door opened, and there stood my mother-in-law, Khadija, with her head covered in a green kerchief and her face bloated and sallow. Her creases had deepened and were visible to the naked eye, and her small lips were dry and pursed, yet the tip of her nose was scarlet, and her eyes were hazy and tumescent as if she hadn't stopped crying for three days.

As soon as she spotted me, she burst into tears and swiftly withdrew, and I wondered if she could no longer stand my sight since I was clearly alive and in excellent health, but her daughter had died forever.

Nonetheless, I was as affected by the loss as she was since I had lost two precious people while she had lost just one. I know she never carried me lightly in her heart, and this riddle has never stopped to perplex me since I did nothing to offend her. But, so far from it, the more I tried to be pleasant and positively respond to all her vagaries— and they were many and diverse—the more I sensed her becoming a tiny satrap. I can't blame her; she's a mother, and Dalila was her one-of-a-kind child.

I entered, though, and politely encouraged the chauffeur to accompany me. Mr Houssine came to greet us. He kissed my cheeks and muttered faintly:

– That's God's will, my son. God's will, may He be compassionate to us! Please come in. It's so bad you couldn't make it to the funerals. The cemetery housed the whole hamlet. All glory to Allah. That is His will, and we shall not resist it, my son.

• • • ● ●• ● • ● • • •

Chapter Three

THE INDIAN SHOWED UP

WE FOLLOWED MR HOUSSINE down the hallway and the little garden, and he led us into one of the four rooms, which I observed were crowded. I didn't know all the guys in the room since they weren't all from 'Ouja, as I suspected, but the others - those who recognised me - rushed over right away to shake hands and console me for the double loss. We sat silently in the same drawing room where I used to have lengthy conversations with Dalila. Nobody talked, and I couldn't break the wordless concentration in which we had taken sanctuary.

• • • ● • ● • ● • • •

That afternoon, I went to the graveyard with Mr Houssine and the driver. Then I learned that Dalila was visiting my ailing mother and had been permitted to stay the night with her when the hamlet was attacked. Standing in the middle of the cemetery under the shade of a palm tree, I felt everyone in 'Ouja had left their homes, stores, and enterprises to come and grieve their dead. The graveyard was on the outskirts of the village. A low white stone wall surrounds it, beyond which agricultural fields extend. I spotted the Islamic Militia members strolling along the fence, rifles on their shoulders, and questioned Mr Houssine:

– Did they come by night?

His tiny brown eyes twinkled in the sunlight, and his lips twitched as he wiped the sweat and dust from his tanned face with a green handkerchief. His face seemed thinner and bonier than it had been a few months previously, and he scowled:

– Who do you mean?

– I mean the killers.

– I'm unsure exactly when, but they probably came at daybreak or earlier. They rushed into the police station and the National Guard Headquarters, killed everyone, and then turned their rage to the stores and shops. They broke the doors with explosives, plundered, looted, and thrashed, while others broke into our homes randomly. They raped, robbed, killed whoever resisted, and rampaged relentlessly for hours. It had been a very long nightmare, my son.

– I'm still baffled about how this could ever happen in a country whose people pray to God five times daily and say there is no God but Allah. Has God abandoned us to those bloodthirsty terrorists?

– Don't blaspheme, son. It's His will. Accept it.

– I accept God, but I don't understand his will. The criminals seem to take advantage of it more than those who pray, fast, and do everything to please God, like you, Mr Houssine. They're the reason we're here.

He remained silent, fixing an

imaginary square between his feet. I asked him:

– Do you think they're who the TV says they are, Mr Houssine?

He pondered. His eyes sank deep into their sockets. He was obviously hesitant, and his hand shook as he reached for the cigarette I was handing him.

– These are the former president's crimes, he said. He did not accept being ejected from power.

– You hesitated.

– No, I didn't. I am certain. The terrorists were dressed in long robes and sandals, with long beards and masks on their faces. They presumably attempted to imply that they are Muslims, but I know they are not. We recognised one of them.

– Really? One from 'Ouja? What's his name?

– No, no, you're misguided. Don't

say such rubbish. The terrorist is from a nearby hamlet, and we know his clan. He was a lieutenant in the previous president's army.

I gave him another cigarette, took one for me, and lit them. I looked around and saw some women weeping on the graves, whereas the men accompanying them displayed perfect, woebegone, vapid faces. In such a sad time, we weren't the best people to gaze at. Some men were seated cross-legged on the matted ground, reading the Quran. I overheard their voices droning pathetically, like a long, lingering complaint. I felt depressed and gloomy, and the sky, vaulting its wistful blue high over our heads, seemed wholly unconcerned by our grief. That smiting coldness and unruffled beatitude irritated me. I told myself, "This is perhaps the hour of the Scoundrel. He is probably enjoying his meagre victory and wandering across the desert, intoxicated on blood, like a lone wolf licking its fangs after the gloomy feast. O Lord! Please assist us at this time. Let us continue to trust in your kindness and mercy.

• • • ● • ● • ● • • •

We spent the day at the graveyard, which was so crowded that it reminded me unavoidably, though inconveniently, of the weekly market that used to gather people every Friday in 'Ouja. Oddly, that day was the first Friday following the slaughter. It was the first Friday in many years that I did not see peddlers and merchants congregating in the public square.

After that, I dismissed the chauffeur. He inquired whether he should return to take me back to the capital, and I informed him that it wasn't required since I'd be driving alone. I thanked him, and he got into the Land Rover and waved to us. The automobile rumbled away, leaving a cloud of dust in its wake. Then I parted ways with Mr Houssine, promising to return and see him as soon as possible.

• • • • • • • • • • •

I went along the dusty streets, wandering aimlessly in the sluggish tottering of the dusk. No children were playing and shouting; no coffee shops were open; no men and youth were playing cards and smoking gurgling nargileh; no women were hurrying muffled in their veils, their mysterious eyes gleaming like colourful rainbows in the forlorn desert of our lives, and their ample gowns floating around them. Instead, abandoned dogs and cats chased remains on the wastebins, and armed young militiamen strolled along the street. They are all strangers to the village and are clearly as taken with the gloom that hangs over it as the locals were. I saw them lazing in little groups of three, four, and five, sombre and sad, dressed in long dishdashas or blue denim, as if they were only promenading to greet the sweet twilight of September. The bulk of them were relatively young, maybe under the age of eighteen. Without their weapons, one would mistake them for schoolboys on a field trip.

They looked at me indifferently, and some even hailed me with the traditional Islamic greeting: "Salam Alaykum!" "Wa Alaykum Assalam," I responded.

They have taken over the National Guard headquarters and the police station, as well as the regular army. However, I only saw a dozen soldiers, one of whom was a sub-officer, and they appeared to be on good terms with the militia. After the armed forces split into two parts, one of them loyal to the scoundrel and the other to the new masters of the country, I thought they had much to do with combating each other. That's why they sent the Islamic militia to maintain order in 'Ouja after the disaster.

When I crossed the main street and engaged in a bifurcated one to join the building where I lived, I saw them chatting on the pavement before the broken gate of 'Ouja Bank. It was just a ten-minute walk from the bank, but I postponed my visit to my mother's house until another day since I was exhausted. I travelled all morning in the scorching heat, then spent the afternoon accepting and delivering condolences and speaking with strangers. I needed a clean wash and a good night's sleep to recuperate. Mr Houssine had tried to keep me for supper, but I politely declined, blaming my indisposition on exhaustion. He didn't insist.

I ascended the steps of my seven-story building to the second level and opened my apartment door. I hesitated for a few minutes at the doorway as if I couldn't quite believe I was back home. "Home?" I muttered to myself, "Where is home now?" The location of a man's birth is not that important. What matters is what a guy does to improve himself and his life. I shut the door and traversed the little hallway to the living room, where I paused for a second in the middle of the room before entering the two other rooms, the kitchen and the bathroom, with the same unplaceable sorrow. It was no good to be back home. I was an outsider in my hometown. The brickwork, furniture and paraphernalia, I could get anywhere. What I can't find now is my family's love and support. Nothing is the same as it was when I left. The tiny Canary had passed away. I discovered its decomposing little body in the cage. Because it hadn't completely rotted, I assumed it died recently. My mother was ill in her last days. Yet, I'm surprised Dalila didn't take the bird to her house.

My mother had undoubtedly given her a key; she could probably go to the apartment and feed the tiny bird. What happened? I feel bad about all this. Nothing was left to comfort me. I won't listen to the chirpy twittering in the morning and evening. I unlocked the cage and held the dried body in my hand; it was exhaling a foul odour. I wrapped it in an old white handkerchief and went out to give it a proper burial in the garden. At least, I'd bury the bird, as I could not attend my relatives' funerals!

Despite my tiredness and gloom, I opened the door and walked down the stairs, the dead Canary in one hand and a little pickaxe in the other. Then, as the swarthy shades of the evening stretched a dark mantle over the households, I got out and walked on the lawn.

Some lights were faintly glinting

through the windows, and I regretted not purchasing a petrol lantern before my incarceration. But how could I know what would unfold in my peaceful village and the whole country? So I dug a pit, buried the small body inside, and then stood in awe of the bizarre series of deaths that had even the animals in shock. Then I returned to the flat, threw the pickaxe in the kitchen closet, removed my clothes, and went to the bathroom.

About a half-hour later, I was still dozing in my bath when I heard someone knocking on the door. I lingered since I wasn't expecting visitors before yelling loudly, standing in my tub:

– Who's there?

– Open up, it's me, said a manly voice, which was not unfamiliar to me, although, in my disconnected mood, I could hardly put a face on it.

I quickly put my bathrobe on and scurried towards the door, wiping the wetness off my body. I noticed that the unexpected visitor's voice had a strange accent. So it could only be my British neighbour, Mr Marmeduke, whom I had not yet seen, although it was unusual for him to knock on my door at night. But then, the voice came over again, this time in English:

– It's me, your good friend, Mr Bassam.

– I knew it was you, I said as I opened the door. I'm glad to see you again, yet I'm stunned. How did you get my address? Please, come in. How are you doing, Mr Abdullah?

The Indian limped in, apologising for the intrusion.

– If you're too busy, I will come back later. I don't like to bother you.

– No, you're not bothering. Let's

drink a cup of tea. You're welcome.

I led him into the living room and urged him to rest while I changed my clothes in five minutes. I saw he was wearing a handgun beneath his belt; when he sat down, he removed it and placed it on the table. Was it heavy, or was it just to show it to me? I returned to the living room a few minutes later, refreshed and dressed lightly in cotton pants and a shirt, and asked him if he liked coffee or tea.

– Please, Mr Bassam, don't bother. I came merely to greet an old buddy and convey my heartfelt sympathies. I heard about what happened to your family and am very sad. Some of our men saw you in the cemetery this afternoon and indicated your house to me. So I came over to share your grief. It was a horrible crime, Mr Bassam, causing unnecessary suffering. Sheikh Mohamed Mashawir and the other brothers assigned me this difficult task. Please, accept our heartfelt condolences.

– Your honest compassion, Mr Abdullah, has touched me. Thank you a lot.

– Not at all. I just wanted you to know you're not alone in your grief. We've all been through similar situations. I'm unsure whether I told you about my hardship in Kashmir, where I lost my father, mother, wife, and children in a terrible and deadly conflict between Muslims and Hindus.

– No, I don't think you ever told me that.

– That's how I decided to join the Islamist Jamaat Party. I had never been a militant before, but when I found myself alone in the world after some fanatical Hindus set fire to the family house during the night while I was far away on business, I had no alternative but to grab firearms and join the Jamaat. Didn't I have to avenge my family? Besides, there was nothing left for me to do but despair. I was working hard to support my family, and I used to travel for business throughout India, Pakistan, and Afghanistan. I wasn't wealthy but made a decent livelihood selling carpets and other handcrafted items for a prominent merchant in Karachi. I cherished two lovely children; my mother and father were still living with us, my wife adored me, and everything was fine. We were saving money to purchase a good property in town since we had just rented the house that caught fire. I would have been living peacefully with my family in Karachi by now; I may have saved enough money to establish my own company instead of travelling from country to country like a rabid hound, constantly with the dreadful death looming over my head or following behind like a shadow. But the ways of Providence are unfathomable, and I have accepted my fate. It's God's will, my brother! The Arabs say it's Mektub! I believe it is true.

There was a brief pause. Then, I excused myself and went to the kitchen, where I heated water and made tea. I returned with the tray, placed it on the table by the handgun, and sat in the second armchair facing the Indian.

Chapter Four

THE NIGHTMARE

I'M SORRY, BUT THERE is no food. As you are aware, I have just returned from the capital and did not...

Abdullah cut me off abruptly:

– Never mind! I've already dined. (He took a breath.) I arrived too late. The scene was dreadful! The ordeal's indicting marks were dispersed over every street, every house, and every corner. They tormented them, raped women and girls in front of their fathers and spouses, and hacked off the latter's genitals when they resisted or killed them. Did you watch the TV news report? It was nothing in comparison to what we discovered when we arrived. - I didn't watch TV.

– I understand. After all, it's your family, your neighbours and your friends.

He took a sip of his tea. I offered him a cigarette, but he respectfully declined. I informed him that I had just become an unrelenting addict, smoking cigarettes as if it had always been my habit. I had finished the packet Suleiman Mughli had given me and purchased two more on my trip to 'Ouja. I lit my cigarette and said:

– It is somewhat soothing. In fact, what happened in this town blew me away. When I was crossing the main street, I noticed the massive damage that had flogged nearly all of the buildings. They had even broken into the bank despite its gate being specially secured. They most likely utilised powerful explosives. It would take a long time for us to repair and fix all of the damage done. But the loss of human lives was even worse. It's a tragedy beyond comprehension. Nothing could justify it.

   – I also believe so. But it's the price of liberty, brother, and it's steep. (He took another pause, drank his tea, and then went to the point behind his unexpected visit:) - Why not join us?

   – The question was surprising, even astounding, since I had not imagined myself strutting about like a boy scout with the Islamist Militia. I pondered. I don't want to anger this guy.

   – I wish I could, but I can't. I apologise. Hassan is expecting me in the capital. We have a lot of work to do.

   He didn't seem impressed.

– The Director of Security, you mean?

– Yes, I said, nodding.

Abdullah made a bored, if not contemptuous, wave with his hand. I immediately expressed my gratitude to Hassan:

– It was he who released me; I owe him my freedom.

My last sentence seemed to irritate the Indian.

– You are misguided, brother. You don't owe him your freedom.

I stared at him, stunned, awaiting an explanation, which he eventually gave after a little pause.

– Hassan isn't as important as you think, said Abdullah. I know a lot about him. You owe him nothing. You are now free because the omnipotent God is merciful to you.

I remained silent. He went on:

– My name is Abdullah, which

means the slave of God, he said. But we are all God's slaves. He owns us, and we owe Him everything, including our lives. Thinking otherwise is not only incorrect but also blasphemous. Hassan's ex-brother-in-law, Mamdouh, the Minister of Interior, is now protecting the Director of Security. However, despite holding a high position in the government, Mamdouh remains very suspect. Before the Revolution, he also held a high-ranking position. There will be a reshuffle in the coming days or weeks. They may both lose their jobs. For the time being, the government maintains them for political reasons. They are needed as a facade to facilitate negotiations between the Islamic State and the European or American governments. We don't want the latter to support our enemy, the scoundrel. That's why

Mamdouh and Hassan, known to have connections with Westerners, are kept in power. It won't be long before they get fired. I don't see them succeeding in their jobs. You need to be very careful. Don't trust them.

Alarm bells sounded in my mind.

– What you said has disturbed me. I assumed that the Emir trusted the Minister and the Director of Security. So, is that not the case anymore?

– No confidence, the Indian snapped. They just happened to be at the right place at the right time, but their good fortune will not last. We have a lot of information on them. Mamduh is a profligate and scandalous pig, as corrupt as a whore. As to his brother-in-law... (He came to a halt, stared at me for a long moment, then said:) Would you give me your word of honour that you will not repeat it to them or anyone in their entourage?

– Of course, you can trust me, Abdullah.

– Well, then, do learn that the pig is not a Muslim.

– What pig? Who are you talking about? Hassan?   The Indian's black eyes were shot with blood, and hatred washed over his face as he replied:

– Yes, Hassan. The pig is neither a Muslim, a Christian, a Jew, nor even a Buddhist since no religion condones what he did.

– I muttered nervously:

– Why? What did he do?

– Do you have no idea? Well, then, listen. The pig has just been sleeping with his stepmother! That is the most heinous sin I am aware of. It's like sleeping with your mother or sister.

He spat, splattering saliva over the cup of tea he was still holding in his hands.

– Oh! Oh, my God! Indignantly, I exclaimed. This can't be true. It's slanderous gossip. I know his family story. He'd never known his mother, and the stepmother was like a second mother to him. She raised him.

–   No,   interrupted   Abdullah stubbornly.   You   know   nothing, sorry! I've   been   in   this   country for   a   little   over   a   year,   and everything I told you came from a trustworthy source. Furthermore, that trustworthy individual is familiar with Hassan and his family because he is one of their neighbours.

– That's   not   a   reason,   I   said, perplexed. He could be wrong. What if he's their neighbour? Is he a member of the same household as them? This is a malicious rumour. I'm sorry, but I don't believe it.

The Indian continued, unmoved and cold-hearted:

– Don't you trust us? Okay, then! You claim he's an orphan, and that lady is like his mother? Very good. You don't know the inside of a guy as well as I do. As soon as his father passed away, Hassan jumped on his stepmother, who was still young and beautiful, and slept with her as if she were her wife, the swine! He committed the great Haram! It's a tragedy, but it's not unthinkable. I know another pair in India, a brother and his sister, who lived together as husband and wife. They'd even had a kid. I assumed they were a happy and normal couple when I first saw them. Until an elderly man who had known the family since they left Calcutta told me their story, I had never considered the possibility of terrible incest. When their parents discovered their incest, they ran away and went to live in Bombay, where I met them. I was as shocked as you are now, and I never returned to see them again. I also know about another pair in Dhaka, but I haven't seen them: an uncle living maritally with his niece after his brother died. However, the girl escaped and reported the incident to the police. He had already committed suicide by the time they arrived. Isn't it just revolting? But what I tell you is true, even if it's never pleasant to talk about it.

• • • • ● • ● • ● • ••

I was still in the labyrinth when he departed, wondering into whose hands I had fallen and what type of wild monsters I was dealing with! I wobbled in the room, clogged and squeezed by a horrible sorrow, subject to a terrible sadness, unable to make sense of what had just happened to me and around me. The Indian, on the other hand, made it clear that the new administration was neither homogenous nor firmly formed on a consistent pattern. Significant disagreements exist among its members, and the fight for dominance is still in its early stages. Thus, I discovered that Mohamed Mashawir, the Chief of the Islamic Militia, is a powerful man with thousands of fanatics at his command. It was obvious that even the regular army, police, and National Guard feared this small force. The Afghans are undeniably ambitious. If he supports the Emir, he wants him to remove people like Hassan and Mamduh from their positions; hence, I assume he has a clear interest in smearing and discrediting his rivals. The Indian did not reveal his sources, but I thought the Afghan was most likely the primary source. Despite his nickname, which implies that he is a foreigner, the Afghan is a citizen of our country who has been hired to fight in Afghanistan as a professional Jihad mercenary. The fact that his family is wealthy made it even more exciting for him. He is the elder son of a well-known trader in the capital. When he was arrested and charged with gun smuggling and attempting to sow sedition, along with the gang who had followed him from Afghanistan, the best lawyers in the country competed fiercely to defend them. Hassan and Mamduh are unquestionably obstacles to such a man's rise to prominence. He has two essential things that will bring him fame or seal his fate: money and power. The sooner he gets rid of his rivals, the better. Apart from the Emir and the Scoundrel, I don't see another man capable of persevering in that ruthless, turbulent, and insidious struggle for power. The Islamic Militia, the third army in the nation (given there are already two battling each other), over which Mohamed Mashawir has noticeable supremacy, is unquestionably the formidable tool he would not hesitate to employ to achieve his goal.

Money is not an issue since he is reportedly a multimillionaire. I do not doubt that he is spreading false allegations about Hassan, and the Indian seems to believe him as if his words were the Koran! When he told me that highly dubious and scabrous story about Hassan's pretended lust, I noticed the parrot pointing out his nib. I don't dispute that such heinous perversions might occur, but why should they happen to Hassan in particular? The conversation with the Indian did not, as he claimed, soothe or console me; on the contrary, it intensified my melancholy and concerns. The country is no longer safe; it has become a death trap for all of us. If I want to live in peace, I must remove my archives. Who can guarantee that the militia will not storm my house and loot it? It would be my feast if they discovered what I was doing before their departure!

I got nothing by helping the King or the President who replaced him, and I have a hazy feeling that I will get nothing more by supporting the current dictatorship. I need to act before it's too late. If I could have placed the archives in my vehicle and driven securely beyond the area, I would have destroyed them that same night. But it was impossible with all those armed men roaming the streets. As a result, I waited until the morning.

. . . • ● • ● • . . .

After months of scary promiscuity, my first night at home was far from comfortable. I felt a little down, and my sleep was disturbed. I dreamed that I was racing through the streets of the capital, tattered and barefooted, while Hassan, the Afghan, the Indian, the Islamic Militia, and all the jail inmates were hounding me like a pack of wolves, shouting:

– Stop the Scoundrel! Catch him! He must be beheaded!

I shouted back to them without

stopping my run:

– I'm not the Scoundrel! This is a mistake! I am Bassam, your friend Bassam.

But my protest was in vain. They continued to pursue me, threatening to decapitate me:

– We'll get you, wicked Scoundrel! Murderer! We'll kill you. Stop. Come back.

I was naked, but a little object wrapped in a white towel was in my palm. I had a firm grasp on it. I turned to look at my pursuers and extended my hand. The little creature in my hand palpitated and soared into the air. It was my canary.

I awoke sweating profusely and simmering like a water kettle. Flustered and bleary-eyed, I rushed to the bathroom and placed my head underwater. When I was refreshed, I thanked God because it had all been a nightmare. What if that horrible dream materialised? What if I were to face such a horde of people, whom I would be the one to lancinate, throw down, and slaughter?

I chose not to worry about it and went to the kitchen to make a nice cup of black coffee, which I drank while smoking two cigarettes. Then I rummaged under my bed and took out the hatbox containing my secret archives. When I found them, I thanked God for a second time. I checked, and they seemed to be intact. Either Dalila or Mum - maybe both - saw them. It seemed doubtful that they did not sweep the dust beneath the bed since they were the only ones who had access to the unit throughout my extended vacation in prison. They would have had no idea what was inside if they had opened the package. I had hidden the secret archives behind a pile of old magazines and newspapers. They would have thought it was just a harmless parcel.

Naive women! How could they anticipate or believe that the whole nation, let alone foreign spies, would pay any amount to get these priceless secret documents? It's a treasure, a true data bank, and a massive computer capable of competing with the most advanced and diligent intelligence agencies! Competing? You've got to be kidding, Mister Bassam! You are fully aware that your archives outnumber any computer's incredible memory! Take, for example, Samir, who had no notion of what was happening in 'Ouja until he came in with great fanfare. He was probably not even born when you began accumulating and storing knowledge on every soul and event in the village and its environs until your archives grew to become 'Ouja's true, unique, and unmatched memory. Even if everyone forgets what happened in a particular year, you can remind them of those joyful or painful days.

I dressed properly and grabbed the heavy box intending to go and burn its contents in the fields beyond the hamlet. But then something unexpected occurred.

Chapter Five

ENCYCLOPEDIA OF 'OUJA

– You're making a serious mistake!

– Eh?!

I came to a complete halt in the middle of the room while pulling the box toward the corridor.

– Where are you going?

Standing at the same spot, I turned around numerous times, but there was no foreign presence in the room. I thought it was one of my crazy angels nosing into my business again. That wouldn't be the first time.

– Who's speaking to me?

– Leave that box in peace, the mysterious voice said. Why do you want to get rid of it?

– Whoever you are, this is none of your business, I replied.

– Be responsible, Bassam. You're an adult, aren't you? You're not a coward. So, don't lose your nerve over such trivial matters. What happened to you? Are you scared of your actions?

– Who... Who... arrrrrr.... you? I shouted nervously.

– Don't shout, son. Be a gentleman. I am your father.

I was startled when I thought I recognised the mysterious voice:

– Dad?

– Yes, young man. I'm here to guide you before you lose yourself.

I was silent for a few seconds.

Fortunately, it was early morning. The light in the room was still dim. But I couldn't see the face of my father. I didn't know what to do. Finally, I tried to say something, gathering my confidence with both hands.

– But I don't see you, Dad. Where are you?

– You can't see me, son. I'm communicating from the other side. Don't be a fool. You have to keep your archives.

I've gotten over my astonishment.

– But, Daddy, you know nothing of what's happening here, I said. You've been absent for a long time. The country has gone insane, and we are in a dramatic situation.

– The country is none of your concern, boy. You aren't going to pretend you're another saviour, are you? There are too many already, and they are all charlatans with the same goal: snatching power to lay their hands on the people's riches. An ignorant people who they can easily control and enslave to their whims. You are not to blame for their disaster. Please stay away from it. The archives you planned to destroy are no longer yours. It is our heritage; it belongs to the future as much as it does to the past. You have no right to squander the past or the future. Your past actions and records are your memories, and your memories are your eyes, kid. If you want to go blind, burn your memories. A man without a past is a man without a future.

With a prickling sensation, I peered dizzily at the big hatbox that had served as my archives for years.

– Instead of destroying it, hide the box in a safe place. If you're worried, never allow yourself to waste it because you'll regret it bitterly later, the voice continued. It would be the same as destroying yourself if you ruined your archives, son. Do you only remember the contents of those documents? Why don't you go over them again to refresh your memory? Now that I've warned you, I wish you the best of luck, son. Take care!

I fiddled in the room for a minute or two, unable to understand what had occurred. Was I talking with my father or to myself? Even though the invisible angels often addressed me, I recognised my dad's distinctive voice with piercing, pitched intonations and unfolded placidity. I couldn't possibly mistake it for another. Despite my flaws, my well-trained ear can tell an authentic voice from a sloppy counterfeit. I was so excited and suddenly motivated that I rushed to open the hatbox while kneeling on the carpet. It was the early morning of my second day in 'Ouja—a calm morning with a clear sky and a bronze light streaming through the glass of my window. A morning like many others I'd seen in this same location, but with something extra, something strange and unusual, which was still a mystery to me.

I rummaged through the box, clearing the old newspapers and magazines that concealed the archives. With the dust and even the spiderweb that had weaved its threads in the corners of the box, which I had to clean out with a wet sponge, it was not an easy chore. Nevertheless, I lit a cigarette and accessed the archives containing as many files as the alphabet. Then, and only then, did it occur to me that my archives did not deserve to be destroyed.

Really! My father is wise! My archives contained firsthand information on the people of 'Ouja, their origins, family trees, names, households, properties, businesses, behaviour, and religion, and I did not omit the geography, the history, and the economy of the village, its potentialities, its traditions, heroes, legends, and so on. In short, my work is a comprehensive study that unquestionably deserves to be labelled scientific. My excellent exploration will enchant and ravish historians and sociologists. I have noticed even trivial details in my notes. I had, for example, depicted the number of hens, cows, sheep, or goats such or such person owned, and when possible, their sizes, weights (approximately sometimes, but often with precision - that is, after a conscientious enquiry), their colours, food, distinctive marks such as the length of their legs, the tint of their muzzles, the shape of their beaks, and any birth trait, without forgetting their sexual life of course. Before writing about all this, I had spent hours and hours researching and reexamining each characteristic and category. It occurs to me now that many authors and researchers should crave this work and wish to have at least half my sense of observation, although, unlike them, I did not gather my notes to make them known to the general public, but rather to keep them hidden from prying eyes. These are terrible secrets that are critical to the survival of my village. (Also, who knows? If the people of 'Ouja seek political independence in the future, they will have a basis for doing so: A History for the Independent State of 'Ouja that goes back 3000 years before Christ and even to the Stone Age.

I also counted and recorded the number of stones and bricks that comprised the walls of certain renowned structures, such as the Mayor's House or the party cell. If only I had enough time, I would have counted the amount of gravel and stones in the streets and the number of leaves on the trees, the birds, and even the stars. Indeed, my archives turned out to be a veritable encyclopaedia of 'Ouja, the only one in the country as far as I know. As a result, it is not surprising that many spies want to see this little wonder of learning.

●●●●●●●●●●

Sitting on the carpet, smoking cigarettes and sipping coffee, I leafed through the files of my incredible archives, remembering men, animals, things, and events that were no longer alive. That's when the idea occurred to me, and I wondered why I hadn't thought of it earlier.

I need a computer, a clever machine like Samir, capable of keeping these archives safe and secure for a long time. It is useful whenever I need to consult it or refresh my memory, aside from the fact that a USB flash is much easier to handle and conceal than a large stack of papers. I don't need a big desktop computer; a laptop will do the job. I can locate the right stuff in a supermarket. It was almost midday, and the archives would stay in peril until I went to the capital and bought the needed computer. First, I had to find a secure place like a secret closet, a cellar, or... or... Then I remembered the attic on the roof, which I used for storing old things. If ever the militia or any hostile force or agents stormed my apartment, it is unlikely that they would also search the attic. I had piled up piles of old furniture between its small walls. Some because I am a grand sentimental, and others because I couldn't sell. Who would buy a ripped-up armchair, a rusted iron table, or a broken-legged chair? My prized hat box would go unnoticed among the dusty crates, heaps of old newspapers, and the rest of that pathetic hocus-pocus. I am still determining how long I'll be in the capital, so I had to get everything in order at home before driving to the city. The Director of Security, his sister, and perhaps, the Medal of National Merit are all waiting for me.

After the ordeal of incarceration and the terrible deaths of my relatives, I am a kind of hero since all victims are called "martyrs" and "heroes" in this country. I am more heroic than Hamda La'war, who mysteriously vanished, for he wasn't seen in his office or the cemetery. I had also noted that the party's cell was as black as coal. The rebels, or terrorists, or whoever they were, had set fire to Hamda La'war's Party's cell, where he used to govern the town as if it were his damned ancestors' property! He was unquestionably the most powerful man in 'Ouja. The former Mayor, whom he ousted and took over, the chief of the police, and the commander of the National

Guard were all under his protective nuclear umbrella. He could get them a promotion and a better salary if he were satisfied or ruin their careers if he wasn't.

. • • ● • ● • • • .

I grabbed the hat box back into my arms, opened the apartment door, and began climbing the staircase. On the way, I ran across Mr Marmeduke, the British schoolmaster whose flat was next to mine. He is now an elderly retiree who lives alone with his dog following the loss of his wife. He had visited our country under British rule and fallen in love with it. He had worked at several schools before settling in this peaceful village. Mr Marmeduke could leave when the British troops left the country but preferred to stay.

The independent Education Ministry had renewed Marmeduke's contract with several other compatriots. He is still strong, with a ruddy face, two blue eyes, a protruding nose, a large mouth, and a benign smile that never leaves his face like the Jocund. His forehead is wide and has deep wrinkles crossing it. However, when I met him on the stairwell, he was not smiling, and I believe it was the first time in years that I did not see the Mona Lisa pointing out from the corner of his mouth.

Before I paused to greet him, his rubicund Spaniel ran towards me, yapping, yelping, wagging his tail, and licking my shoes with clear delight. But, of course, I was not surprised by such a warm welcome because I used to have tea with his master on occasion, and on these occasions, I never forgot the dog. And he had probably wondered where all those little delicacies I used to give him had gone during the long months of my absence!

The old schoolmaster appeared depressed and dismal. His glistening blue eyes revealed more than he wanted to.

– I am delighted to see you again, Mr Bassam, and I am deeply sorry for your losses. My heartfelt condolences on the deaths of your mother and your fiancée.

We exchanged handshakes, and I thanked him. I placed the box on the step and noticed right away that he was inquisitive about its contents, though he was too courteous to ask. To avoid any unintended consequences from a misplaced indiscretion or misunderstanding, I hastened to explain:

  – These are old family papers that my mother will no longer need. I will store them in the attic until I see what to do with them.

  – I understand, Marmeduke said. We lost a very kind woman, sadly! I hadn't seen her in nearly a month, and she wasn't alone; the young lady was with her. When I inquired about you, they stated that the lawyer was attempting to gain your conditional release. I see that he has finally succeeded. I am as pleased for you as I am sorry for them.

  I didn't want to inform him that the lawyer accomplished nothing to get me released because it would have been a pointless conversation.

  – Thank you, Mr Marmeduke. The lawyer is capable;   I would have moulded in jail without his assistance. Mr Aroussi is still there.

Once again, I have spoken more than necessary, despite my desire to keep the conversation brief! Marmeduke, who had learned to speak Arabic, wished to know more. He had likely met Mr Aroussi, but he had also gotten used to hearing about the bank during our tea breaks. So he inquired:

– I heard some gossip, but I wonder if it's true. What exactly are his charges?

– I'm not sure, either. I believe he is charged with illegal dealing in foreign currencies.

– Really? That's what I heard as well. It seems absurd to me. Bankers' entire business revolves around interacting with foreign countries and currencies. Isn't this more of a political issue? Something faked by his enemies to bring him down?

– Perhaps, Mr Marmeduke, perhaps! We'll see the end of it in the next days, won't we? I'm sorry, but I won't be able to keep you much longer.

– I kneeled to get my box. Good day, Mr Marmeduke. I'll see you later.

We parted.

An hour later, after I had hidden my box in the attic beneath a pile of old magazines, I finished shaving and was about to leave the flat. I heard a soft knock on the door. I assumed it was the Indian again, and I resolved to get rid of him right away. I wanted to avoid hearing his pretentious homilies and sermons again and wasn't interested in joining the Islamic Militia. I answered the door, expecting to see the Indian, but instead, it was Mr Marmeduke standing before me, alone. The Jocund was smiling.

Chapter Six

HAVOC

– I apologise for bothering you, said Marmeduke. Do you have five minutes?

– Please come in.

He appeared to have something essential to communicate. He would not have disturbed me for a social chat. He followed me into the living room. I offered to sit, but he declined, saying, "I won't stay."

– We can sit down and talk. There is no rush. I was going shopping.

– I'm in trouble, he said. All I need is to talk to someone I trust. With all those strangers on the streets, you get it. I've never seen such an armada in such a small town. He flopped in the armchair. I sat motionless in front of him. After a little pause, I asked him:

– Are you afraid?

– Afraid? No, no. I've been in 'Ouja for about ten years, and everyone knows who I am. Mr Bassam, I'm not scared; I'm worried. It's not just because of the slaughter but also because of what I recently learned from a reliable source in the South.

That was intriguing to hear. For now, the South is a strange land, and I am very anxious about its news. I offered Mr Marmeduke a cigarette and lit another for myself, although I knew he was a pipe smoker. He didn't miss the strange new habit that has altered my behaviour. He said:

– I see you're smoking now!

– Yes, thanks to the jail! I replied with a smile.

His face became sad again as he puffed the smoke from his nostrils.

– The situation could be more transparent, could it not? Of course, you know what they're saying after three days of silence.

I nodded quietly.

– Yesterday, I drove to the neighbouring town, where I know some friends, he continued. We discussed it, and they all seemed convinced that the... um... Scoundrel... well, you know who I mean, will lose the war. So, what he did in 'Ouja - if he did it - was more of a show of despair than an attempt to seize power by sowing terror.

He stopped again. As I remained

silent, he continued:

– However, as you know, I have some acquaintances in the South. Didn't I already tell you about David?

– Yes, you did. He's the oil engineer married to your wife's niece.

– Precisely. I called David, and guess what.

I had no idea. So I sat motionless, waiting for the rest.

– Well, he continued, even though we couldn't talk freely on the phone, David made me understand without saying it plainly that... um... the former president may not be the culprit. Indeed, David could be mistaken, but it's unlikely, for he knows where the scoundrel's troops are based. And most of all, it is unnecessary to mention that Islamists surrounded them and blocked the roads because they had taken control of several villages and towns. So how could terrorists under the scoundrel's leadership possibly move freely and reach 'Ouja, which is far from their southern location? It's true that they have a significant advantage. Their aircraft is operational, and they control the entire oil industry. But then, if they wanted to bombard 'Ouja, it would have been much easier to launch a raid and then justify it with a concentration of enemy troops or something else. In any case, David and his colleagues would have noticed if the scoundrel's troops had relocated to the north, or at least some of them. Yet, this isn't the case. Otherwise, the assailants would not have come from the desert.

I was dumbfounded and confused. But I did not utter a word.

– I'm afraid the thing is more complicated than it appears, Marmeduke said after a little pause.

You know that many Westerners live and work in the South. Most are British, French and Americans, sometimes with their partners and children. Western governments have not interfered so far and will not interfere as long as the oil business stays unharmed. But how long will this condition last? Furthermore, there will be global reactions to what happened in 'Ouja. The American warships are already moored in the bay, according to David.

I dared to ask:

– Will there be an intervention?

– David didn't say anything, but it should be expected, soon or late, if oil transportation is threatened or halted, and the fighters continue to slaughter civilians as they did in this town.

– I thought there was a blockade, though.

– No, that's a rumour. Our ex-"Beloved President" priority is continuing oil production and exportation. He no longer controls the capital but still has a strategic asset: oil. (Pause). That's a damn good leverage in this conflict. I am not optimistic, though. I'm curious what the ex-"beloved President" will do if he believes there is no prospect for him to cross the desert and re-conquer the country. The Islamists are powerful, well-organised, and settling in for a lengthy reign. If the Scoundrel loses his nerve, he can blow up the wells and the entire oil infrastructure. Then, for a long time, we will bid farewell to peace.

– How could he lose his cool? Westerners are said to back him.

– They did that when he was in charge because he promised reforms. But he lied to them and his people. So, it's different now. They will not help him. A man in despair is neither sensible nor clever. The Westerners had tuned up for many years with the former king, who was very conservative, although less fanatical than the present government. However, ideology may become a minor subject of discord if crucial Western interests are guaranteed. The question that needs an answer is: how much disposed is the current government of the Islamic State to give those required guarantees? The former "Beloved President" is no longer trustworthy. The controversy over the lurid trafficking of white women had done nothing to improve his image. The press is reporting on his probable ties to the international Mafia. All of this isn't very tidy or clean. Nonetheless, unlike the local media, no one media outlet in Europe referred to him as the 'butcher' of 'Ouja. Perhaps they will in the coming days, but there has been no evidence of his involvement thus far, despite what the Islamists claim.

He paused. We could hear an ambulant merchant shouting and a bicycle ringing through the open window of the sitting room. The terrifying tragedy gradually succumbed to life; the village was wiping away its tears and striving to continue its daily fight for survival.

– Is that your opinion as a witness? I asked Marmeduke. Have you got any clue what the culprit's genuine identity is?

He pondered.

– I'm not sure. Both parties could have perpetrated the massacre for different reasons. But don't you believe the Islamists have a bigger interest in it? They badly need foreign neutrality to crush their local rival, and such an episode may discourage Western nations from providing help to the Scoundrel.

– Do you assume they allowed such a thing only to prevent the Scoundrel from getting Western support? I asked, surprised by such a thought that had not occurred to me. You already said he lied to them and lost credibility!

– Yes, he did. But the Scoundrel is nice compared to the Islamists, who seem dedicated to destroying the West, leaving Westerners no choice other than to convert to Islam or accept enslavement. Isn't it obvious, Mr Bassam? Furthermore, the country is in a state of chaos. We don't know who is leading. We don't know whether this new "Emir of the believers" is the real leader of the organisation or just a dummy. Then who is hiding behind the curtains and manipulating the actors on the stage? We cannot yet answer, Mr Bassam, but one thing is certain. Those who organised the massacre in 'Ouja are not the former president's men. The latter may be a dictator with many flaws, but he is not a political fool. He understands the importance of having Westerners on his side.

I was shocked.

– Mr Houssine, my father-in-law, told me the exact opposite. He was certain that one of the soldiers who attacked the town was a sub-officer in the Scoundrel's forces.

– Maybe he was. He could be a deserter who switched camps.

– Had they arrested him?

– No, unfortunately!

– This only proves one thing. Some men who participated in the massacre are very familiar with this village.

Such a possibility was not out of the question. The sub-officer could have been deployed to confuse. Nonetheless, I was reluctant to believe the new regime had orchestrated the slaughter. Why did they wait three days before announcing the news? Mr Marmeduke was also perplexed by the silence, and he agreed with me that since the men of the new regime had a clear interest in publicising the horrible genocide, it was both paradoxical and unwise for them to wait all that time before making it known to the public in the country. When we parted, we were both in the most perplexing maze.

• • • • ●•● • ● • ••

I had planned to take Zerga, my blue automobile, for a ride around the town. But Zerga was reticent to leave the damp shade of the parking after nearly six months of forced idleness. Its engine coughed and sneezed as I turned the ignition key, and that was all I got. So instead, I decided to go for a walk.

As I walked out, I saw the young Khaled and some of his friends gathered on the pavement in front of the building. They greeted me, and I asked if they could assist me. They couldn't say no, even if my captivity had ruined my reputation. They were ready to follow me back to the parking because they still recalled those beautiful days - oh, long gone!—when we used to attend football matches together.

I sat behind the wheel as they surrounded Zerga and pushed the old car forward. It coughed and sneezed again but was eventually forced to act as expected of a real automobile. I thanked them and hit the speed pedal with my foot. I went on a tour of the village to assess the extent of the devastation, stopping here and there to buy a fuel lamp and some food from the shopkeepers.

The mess of destruction astounded me. Some stores were broken; their doors were smashed, their glass windows were shattered, and their furniture was lacerated. I felt extremely sorry for Mehrez, the grocer whose business had been utterly wrecked.

– Look what those criminal sons of a bitch did, Mr Bassam, he groaned as I stopped by his shop. They ruined me; they destroyed my life. They left nothing safe after their passage!

I peered through the door. I didn't dare enter. So awful was the disaster! Mehrez's son, roughly nineteen years old, was attempting to bring order to the anarchic shop. It was upsetting to witness. The commodities were scattered across the floor and mounded in an unbelievable jam. The sugar melted with olive oil and rice, pepper with salt and flour, coffee with spaghetti and marmalade, soaps with shattered bottles of various liquids, and the aggressors had even defecated on the counter. It was carnage.

– They didn't just steal money, Mr Bassam. They rampaged like beasts. This is insane! This is inhumane! Simply inhumane!

Meanwhile, his barber neighbour,

Mustapha, had joined us, and upon hearing this complaint, he commented:

– Consider yourself lucky since they didn't kill you!

– Would they hesitate if I had been in the shop? No, Mustapha. They wouldn't. Those sons of a bitch are monsters who cut babies' throats. I envy Mr Bassam, for he was safe in prison.

– Don't be stupid, said the barber. You just lost money and goods, and they can be replaced. But he lost his mother. How, for God's sake, will he ever be able to replace her? Don't you have any brains, Mehrez?

– Yes, I know, the grocer said. I'm sorry, Mr Bassam. Please accept my heartfelt apologies and sincere condolences.

Before I could respond, Mustapha quickly added:

– And Miss Dalila, his fiancée, may Allah be merciful to both.

The two men then hugged me, and I thanked them. Mehrez commented after a pause:

– I am utterly sorry, Mr Bassam. With all the dead we had buried, I can no longer remember who passed and who survived. I'm even more surprised now when I encounter someone I believe dead! It is not the staggering number of fatalities that strikes me, but rather the survivors. I'm still puzzled about why they stopped short of exterminating the entire town!

– They won't fail to exterminate us next time, the barber predicted sarcastically.

– They'll almost certainly start by cutting your throat, retorted the grocer, irritated. What's with your sinister raven croaking? Is it because they didn't go near your damned shop?

– You should thank God for sparing your life when half the village was slaughtered, Mustapha said. Instead, you're still whining about losing two bottles of mineral water and some soap! You should think about it, lad. They did not hurt me because the Quran protected my shop. Besides, I give to the poor and am not a miser!

Mehrez became enraged by this response and yelled, spraying us with saliva:

– You aren't a miser! What exactly do you mean? Who is the penny-pincher? Then you see nothing of this mess! Would you be happy if they slit my throat?

– It's not what I mean, the clumsy barber said. Why should I be happy? You are my brother. But I wouldn't have been surprised if they did. Many people were killed, but you can still do your business as if nothing had happened. Look at Mr Bassam; what did he get for all his trouble and losses? Nothing! The deaths of his mother and fiancée are far more devastating than all of your losses combined. That is why I believe you should consider yourself fortunate, and I am not mistaken.

Mustapha glanced at me, maybe looking for support, but I remained silent. Then Mehrez looked at me and said:

– Now is not the time for that kind of discussion. It would help if Mustapha showed more empathy for the suffering of others and spared us his recriminations.

The barber said, "Salam Alaykum," taking leave and walking away towards his store.

· · · ● ● · ● · · · ·

Chapter Seven

THE ONE-EYED BOSS VANISHES

Mehrez shook his big head as if still reprobating his neighbour's lack of tact, and his chubby face, almost barred by a huge and long schnozzle, became pink as he said:

– I had been a trifle hard on him. I'm afraid he became enraged, but he's always dipping his muzzle in the wrong place! I wasn't complaining. I only expressed my anger at such an unnecessary mess, Mr Bassam. After all, the dead are our bigger family. I am not heartless. By Allah, your mother is also my mother! On the other hand, Mustapha is the last person who can lecture me on my behaviour. He didn't lose a single dime in the shambles. He is the lucky one, not you or me. Nonetheless, he dares to preach to me as if I were insensitively apathetic to the disaster that struck the entire town. But it wasn't just my shop that they destroyed; it was also the bank - your bank, Mr Bassam. All the money I had saved for years on your advice, all the money I now need to restart my business, has suddenly vanished. Fiffffff! Nothing was left to us, you understand? They stole our money, ruined our businesses, raped women, and slaughtered everyone. They left us broke, devastated, and crushed.

The culprit, scoundrel or not, is still alive, and no one will reimburse us.

He burst into tears. The sight of this strong man sobbing on the threshold of his wrecked shop, like an orphan child, depressed me to no end. I attempted to calm him down.

– Don't let hopelessness take over your mind, Mehrez. This is God's will. Furthermore, this is not the first disaster to strike the country. You may have some memories of other calamities, natural or man-made. The war for independence, for example, was bloody and cruel.

He brushed his tears away and answered:

– No, Mr Bassam, sorry, but it wasn't like this.

I looked at him dumbfounded. He went on:

The Britons killed or imprisoned the nationalists who fought and killed their soldiers. That's war. They were, after all, protecting themselves. We battled them because we desired independence. So it was kill or accept to be killed. Yet, the conflict had a sense of purpose for them or us. Now, look at what we've done with our independence! Is this a fair and legitimate struggle? Is it just, logical, and acceptable that we slay each other simply because we disagree on power-sharing or the regime kind? What about individuals who have no interest in politics? What about the women and children who have no idea who are the bastards controlling this horrible country? Is this our independence and sovereignty, Mr Bassam? Is this our freedom? Is this even what our religion teaches? If this is the case, I wish we stayed under British rule. Because if this is the free country for which so many martyrs have given their lives, then let them hang me for betraying such freedom - the freedom to accept enslavement to a local thug.

– I understand your outrage, Mehrez, but please calm down. The walls have ears.

I looked around, terrified, and noticed a lorry of the Islamic Militia passing by. It was carrying a dozen armed men. The coffee shop had opened on a street corner, and a few customers were sipping their drinks on the terrace. Other merchants and traders have opened their shops. Children had gathered to witness the wreckage, and the men yelled aggressively at them, threatening to beat them with a stick. They dispersed and ran down the street like a flock of scared birds.

– Let them hear, said the grocer. I mean that they hear me. What should

I worry about? What would I lose more than I lost? Where were they when the terrorists massacred the village? They are now heroes and saviours! Hah! Who the hell are they? Where did they come from? Who invited them? Where are the police and the regular troops? They sent us a militia! We are tired of those inept rulers, their greed, corruption, lies, and hypocrisy, Mr Bassam. I express what I think, and if they want to jail me or kill me, let them do it. I'm not better than those who died.

– Calm down, Mehrez. You'll be reimbursed anyway.

– How? When? By whom? Who will ever care about us? They are busy fighting each other for a chair that they will not keep more than others kept before them, and they are making of their people, a people of victims, a flock of sheep that they lead to the slaughterhouse. And they call themselves leaders! Tfuh!

He spat on the ground. The poor man was in despair. He clung to my words, and his eyes twinkled.

– I believe you'll get help; be patient.

– I'll be patient. God will help us. We only expect help from Allah.

After a minute of silence, he asked:

– Will they compensate us for these damages?

– Perhaps not for everything, but whatever comes will be helpful.

– I trust you, Mr Bassam. But... He grinned, moving his head in a tired gesture. I no longer have faith in our rulers. If we exclude human lives, the value of what was lost in 'Ouja, could be estimated only in millions, not thousands. How would they fairly compensate everyone? Even if they give me a quarter of my losses, it won't fully recover my business. It's too sad! I'm done, my brother. Well done!

  – Be faithful, Mehrez. Allah is great and generous, you know.

  – Yes, he responded tiredly. Great and generous!

. . . .

  When I left Mehrez, I got into my car to continue my explorative ride around the town. When I passed by the bank, I realised I had also lost my deposit and savings in the robbery. However, I was less worried than Mehrez. Unlike him, I was confident that the head office in the capital would compensate all 'Ouja customers and local staff. I pulled out near the pavement. A group of armed men were standing before the bank. Without turning off the ignition, I stared at the shredded iron bars of the main gate or what was left of it. It was dark. The explosion had undeniably destroyed a large portion of the lobby and caused an enormous gap in the wall. I could see the burned furniture, the blackened stones, the broken glass, and the papers dispersed on the floor until the doorway. I tried to imagine the state of my office and felt a terrible twinge in my stomach. Mehrez is right. I was safe in prison. Could I have stood passively watching my mother or Dalila being molested without reacting? I have no idea how I should have reacted. Even in my worst nightmares, such a scenario was unimaginable. Nonetheless, I would not have stood watching the massacre from my windows. It was almost daybreak when all of this occurred. I would have known or guessed. I don't have any guns at home, but my father's house still has the old hunting carbine adorning the wall of the sitting room. When I was a kid, I accompanied my father to hunting parties, and I had a lot of pleasure running behind the dog after the hares and birds that were shot down. I did not learn to shoot since I was too young to wield a rifle, and when I reached twenty, I was also exempted from military service because, as my father had retired, I was regarded as the family support. I had to work at the bank to help my parents. Therefore, I remained clueless about firearms. However, I believe it is not difficult to take a carbine and shoot down an aggressor, as I witnessed my father doing to hares and birds many years ago, provided I could find the munitions. If

I happened to be in the house when they broke in, I believe I could have killed those monsters. That's what Abdullah, the Indian, expected me to do when he recommended I join their militia. That is also what Hassan emphasised when he encouraged me to take revenge. However, I must first find the murderers, and even if I did, would I be able to kill them cold-bloodedly? I am not violent and do not believe taking my enemy's life will provide me with any consolation.

I was lost in my thoughts, staring wistfully at the damaged bank, until one of the armed men approached the car and yelled:

– What are you waiting for? It's not a parking spot here, so leave.

His rough voice disturbed my reverie. I apologised.

– I'm sorry, young man. I was just thinking about the terrible events.

– You have nothing to do here. Now, please drive away.

The young militia's erratic mood, and the nervosity of his fingers manipulating the rifle and pointing its cannon to the street to indicate the way, heightened my irritation. I turned the wheel and restarted. It is never a good idea to get these militiamen worked up. They are far more ready to shoot than they are to converse. They would shoot in the air for any minor occurrence and for nothing, either to warn bystanders or simply for the thrill of it. If I hadn't assumed they were natives of this country, I would have believed they were an invading army. Their peculiar behaviour was not that of rescuers or sympathetic aiders but rather that of strangers who, if not tightly controlled by their commanders, would have likely gone on the rampage. I was surprised to see them occupying half of the coffee-shop terrace chairs, playing cards and beaming as if nothing had occurred. It was almost indecent, and the waiter's glum expression was eloquent in telling anyone silently that he was unhappy to serve them. I had planned to take a short break at the coffee shop, but when I saw what was going on, I changed my mind.

I made the decision to visit Hamda La'war at home because I was curious about his apparent absence and assumed that, if he was not himself among the dead, he had lost a family member. And because I was on my way to visit my mother's house, I would stop to inquire about Hamda.

• • • • ● • ● • • • •

I drove through the dusty, tiny alleys of 'Ouja, battered by the September sun, whose rays were lounging on the white roofs and lingering on the swooping palms. Some elderly men in long robes and turbans sat in the shade beneath the walls of their homes, smoking cigarettes or nargileh and staring blankly out the windows while the ragged barefooted children played their innocuous games. The road was humpty dumpty, and the tarmac was in bad shape.

I had to drive carefully and cautiously to avoid the enormous holes, stones, and the little boys darting here and there without warning. Driving through the back streets of 'Ouja has always been difficult. I'm not sure why, despite the residents' repeated requests, the town council was never able to get these roads properly tarred and asphalted. It's as if they're speaking to deaf ears. Some would argue that the budget allotted to the Council's various projects is insufficient! In any case, it will never be enough. The Council's "various projects" mostly consist of the construction of big, luxurious villas for its perpetual members. Since Hamda La'war took over, nothing much has changed. He has always been an important member of the Council, if not the most important. Many said Hamda was the De Facto Council president, although he allowed another dummy to bear this honorific and pompous empty title for the sake of appearances. Finally, he decided to remove him and made sure that nobody could rival him in the council elections, which he won. Hamda was the only candidate for the position.

But if the Mayor and Chief of the Party's cell didn't care about the state of our streets, it's just as well because his new villa on the outskirts of the town was nearly finished. He'd be moving in shortly, so why should he care about the back streets? In any case, the people there are used to living with dusty, humpty-dumpty, muddy roads, mud in winter, and mosquitoes in summer! Thus, Hamda believes that they are not unhappy and that their complaints are merely irrational. If an unlucky, clumsy guy happens to bring up this matter in front of him, the sky will fall on his head. The grumbler will be so ridiculed and humiliated that he will be unable to look his neighbours in the eyes for days. Then Hamda would seize the opportunity to launch one of his famous recriminatory diatribes.

– Look at me, lad! Since you first met me, I've been residing on the same street amid the mud, filthy trash cans, mosquitoes, flies, and other pests. Did you ever see or hear me lamenting? Absolutely not. I do own a car, but I had to work hard to get it. Yes, I am building another house, but it is also the result of my labour. I am a worker, just like you and everyone else in this hamlet, and I will unquestionably prefer to live in a less filthy, more sanitary atmosphere. Despite the fact that I am wealthy enough to live in the capital, I will not forsake my hometown. The funding allotted to this Council is insufficient to cover the costs of maintaining all our streets in good condition. We need to make painful choices because we have many projects. The main street is the town's facade, and it is important. If it is not looked after daily and regularly, we will lose face and a lot of money. Tourists will not visit our town. We now have a hotel. It will stay empty. Those who work at the hotel, men or women, may lose their jobs, and with them also, merchants and traders will be forced to close down due to a lack of customers. What should we do? Fixing all the backstreets or building more hotels t attract tourists? We also need them to see nice villas when they come, not filthy and poor backstreets. What to do about the mud? Well! Let it dry in the sun. Tourists never come in winter but in the summer. They won't see it. We must bring them from Europe, even if it means devoting our whole budget to the upkeep of the main street. I am sorry for the residents dwelling on the back streets, but we do have some priorities. We'll fix what we can in due time, provided we have the budget we are asking for. The local farmers and their workers simply do not grasp that their carriages and animals are the sources of a terrible waste of the taxpayer's money. We repaired a street today. On the morrow, we'll find it has returned to its previous state. It's pointless to continue. What should we do? Forbid the passage of animals and carriages? I warn you. That's what's going to happen if you ask me again to fix the back streets. We also have many other projects. The sanitary structure is deteriorating. We'll experience a shitstorm next winter if we don't fix the gutters and drains. Don't laugh, lads; isn't it your shit? Some of those jerks now appear to assume that I am using the Council's budget to build my own house! Oh, my goodness! If it is a joke, it is bad enough! And if it is not, I warn you. I will sue anyone who accuses me of dilapidating public funds. They don't say it directly to my face because they're shitting cowards, but I know what they're muttering in the dark corners. I got every word they said. I have ears and eyes. Stop talking! I'm not referring to you, morons! You are members of the Council, and you are just as accountable as I am. I'm referring to those jerks who should be aware that I am wealthy and wealthy enough to build six houses if so is my desire. I don't pick in your pockets. I've made no money from working at the cell or the Council. Allah is my witness! I am a God-fearing man. What did my political responsibilities bring me but stress and animosity? Do you believe

I am emotionally invested in these posts? If I had the option, I would not stay for another hour. But the people of 'Ouja want me here, at the head of their Party's cell and their Council. What should I do? Furthermore, I am well acquainted with the major party leaders. I appreciate their support. I wasn't decorated for nuts, but for my heroic deeds as a nationalist militant, you know. My home, my family, and everything in my life is the Party and the Council. Those who believe otherwise should now raise their hands and speak up. I'd want to know what they have in their hearts.

Nobody would raise a hand, move, breathe, or utter a single word unless it was to launch a panegyric speech extolling Hamda La'war's qualities and long-standing dedication to his fellow citizens and the entire nation.

• • • ● ● • ● ● • • •

Hamda was not at home when I arrived. His wife informed me that he had left after the last coup.

– Gone away? You don't mean he is...?

I did not complete the question. But the woman anticipated:

– No, he isn't dead. He went off well before that.

Perplexed, I asked again:

– But where?

She lingered, unsure. I could see her struggling in a predicament. Would she or wouldn't she say? What if I wasn't on their team? She couldn't be aware of my secret agreement with the Director of Security. But, on the other hand, I have no idea what she thought of me.

She was standing in the doorway, her face half-muffled in a wide scarf, while one of her children was clutching her long skirt firmly and yowling. She stooped to take him in her arms, and he stopped wailing. I saw his puffed little caterpillar face, saturated in tears, emerging from the shadows, which reminded me of his one-eyed father's odd facade.

– I don't know, she finally said.

She's lying, I thought.

– He never talks about his business at home.

– No problem, ma'am. I hope he and the rest of your family are safe.

– Thank you for your visit, she said. We're fine, Al- Hamdu Lillah!

She wanted to shorten the talk, so I didn't insist. I bid her goodnight and returned to my car.

While driving to my father's house,

it occurred to me that Hamda could not have vanished without at least warning his wife or informing her of the location where he intended to seek refuge and how she would contact him. Without a doubt, the new regime went after him. I'm aware that the witch-hunt has started. Many former regime officials had been arrested and, following hasty sentences in improvised courts, sent either to jail or beheading execution. If Hamda was ever captured, I am sure he would be sentenced to death. Fortunately, whoever set fire to the party's cell inadvertently spared my life. I know Hamda had a list of his agents and informers in his office, and I wouldn't be surprised if he also had some reports in his drawers. The fire that destroyed the cell freed me of any suspicion... at least in my town.

I'm a new man in 'Ouja now. My past

is as white as a winding sheet. I am a fish in the big sea, a newborn. The air and light of 'Ouja have become vital components of my metabolism, as have the muddy backstreets and the patient and sluggish residents, the palm trees, birds, animals, and stones. Of course, death and sorrow exist. But we must forget and deal with whatever comes our way. Yet, we also must learn to live with our wounds and the memory of our ordeal.

Stay Tuned...
Part III is coming next.

www.ingramcontent.com/pod-product-compliance
Lightning Source LLC
Chambersburg PA
CBHW061217210726
48294CB00006B/1872